INVISIBLE LIZARD IN LOVE

Kurt Cyrus and Illustrated by Andy Atkins

PUBLISHED BY SLEEPING BEAR PRESS

For Linnea and Tina
—Kurt and Andy

Text Copyright © 2019 Kurt Cyrus
Illustration Copyright © 2019 Andy Atkins
Design Copyright © 2019 Sleeping Bear Press

Sleeping Bear Press™

2395 South Huron Parkway, Suite 200, Ann Arbor, MI 48104
www.sleepingbearpress.com
© Sleeping Bear Press

Printed and bound in China.
10 9 8 7 6 5 4 3 2 1

Library of Congress Cataloging-in-Publication Data
Names: Cyrus, Kurt, author. | Atkins, Andy, 1958- illustrator.
Title: Invisible lizard in love / written by Kurt Cyrus ; illustrated by Andy Atkins.
Description: Ann Arbor, MI : Sleeping Bear Press, [2019] | Summary: "After
his jungle friends find their mates, Napoleon the chameleon searches for
his own true love"— Provided by publisher.
Identifiers: LCCN 2019004060 | ISBN 9781534110151 (hardcover)
Subjects: | CYAC: Chameleons—Fiction. | Friendship—Fiction. | Jungles—Fiction.
Classification: LCC PZ7.C9973 Ip 2019 | DDC [E]—dc23
LC record available at https://lccn.loc.gov/2019004060

Napoleon the chameleon loved his spiffy limb.

He loved blending in with every moss, fern, and fungus that grew on it.

He loved his friends, too.

When Mike and Polly came to play, the spiffy limb shook with fun.

It seemed that the laughter would never stop.

But it did stop, the day Mike met Mooka.

"*Eee! Ooo!*" said Mike.

He totally flipped, and off they tumbled on monkey business.

Then Polly met Pedro, and the two chattering parrots flapped away in search of seeds.

"What about *me?*"
asked Napoleon.

The lizard plopped onto the moss.
"Monkeys have monkeys," he said.
"Parrots have parrots.
Lizards have no one."

He scratched a big
lonely heart into the moss.

Then he scratched his initial inside the heart.
His thoughts wandered
as he scratched and scratched.

This went on for days.

Then . . .

Crack! went the rotten old limb.

"Uh-oh," said Napoleon.

SNAP!

Down he went.

Zip! Zip!

Branches whipped by in a blur.

The seventh limb slowed Napoleon down . . .

WHAP!

. . . and number eight stopped him.

Moss and bark rained from the sky.
Fern fronds fluttered by.

A warty lumpstool fell onto
the far end of the branch.

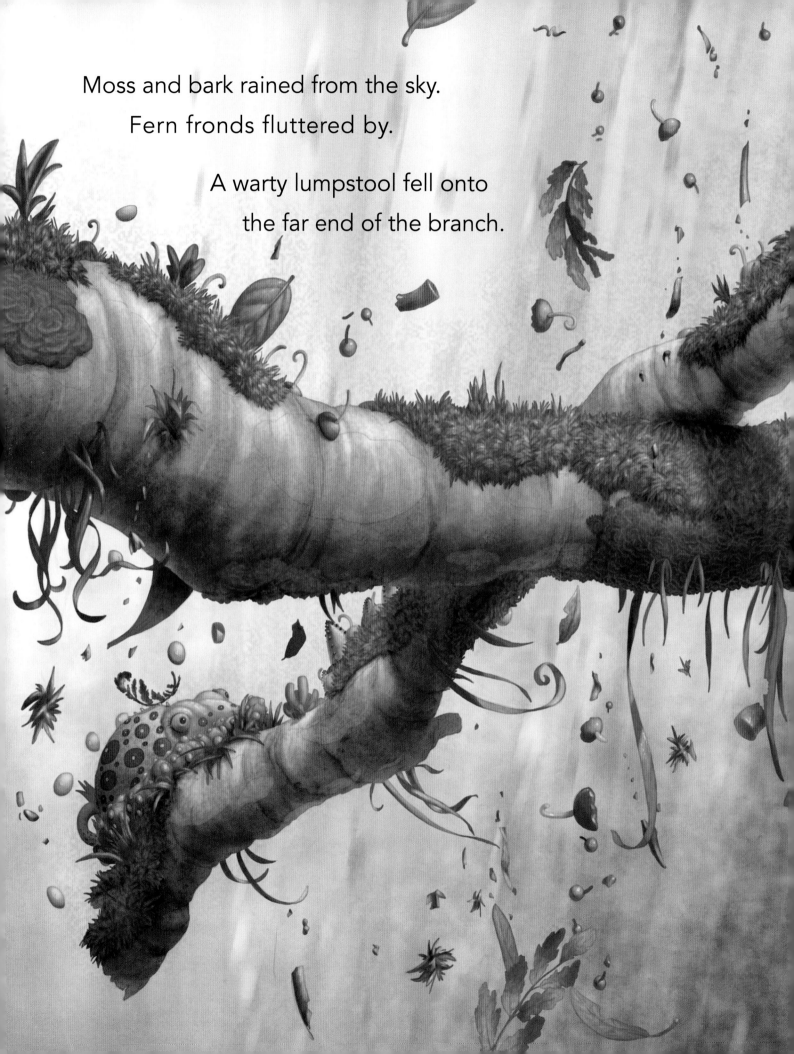

Napoleon held on.

"Well, here's a fine mess," said Napoleon.
"The only thing keeping the limb balanced
is that big warty lumpstool."

"Are you referring to me?" said a lizard on the lumpstool. "I prefer to be called Josephine."

"Yikes!" said Napoleon. "A *girl!*"

It was a fine mess indeed.

When Napoleon moved, the limb teetered one way.

When Josephine moved, it tottered the other way.

"Stop squirming," said Josephine.

"Stop squirming," said Napoleon.

"Stop it!" said Josephine.

"Stop it!" said Napoleon.

"Stop mimicking me!" said Josephine.

"Well, excuse me for being a chameleon!" said Napoleon.

Josephine had an idea.

"Let's both inch forward at the same time. Go very, very slowly."

"No problem," said Napoleon,

who did *everything* very, very slowly.

They each took half a step.
The limb stayed level.

Josephine took another step.

"Hey!" called Napoleon. "Where did you go?
Don't leave me here!"

"Look closely," said Josephine.
"I'm in the whiffle blister bud."

Napoleon blushed. "I knew that."

They kept on creeping.

Down went the sun.

"You should wear sunset colors more often," said Josephine.
"They look really good on you."

"And you make a pretty good evening star," said Napoleon.

Napoleon and Josephine met in the middle of the branch just as sunrise sparkled on the dew.

"You never told me your name,"
said Josephine.

"Napoleon," said Napoleon.

The seesaw branch was an instant hit with the monkeys.
The parrots liked it, too.

Up!

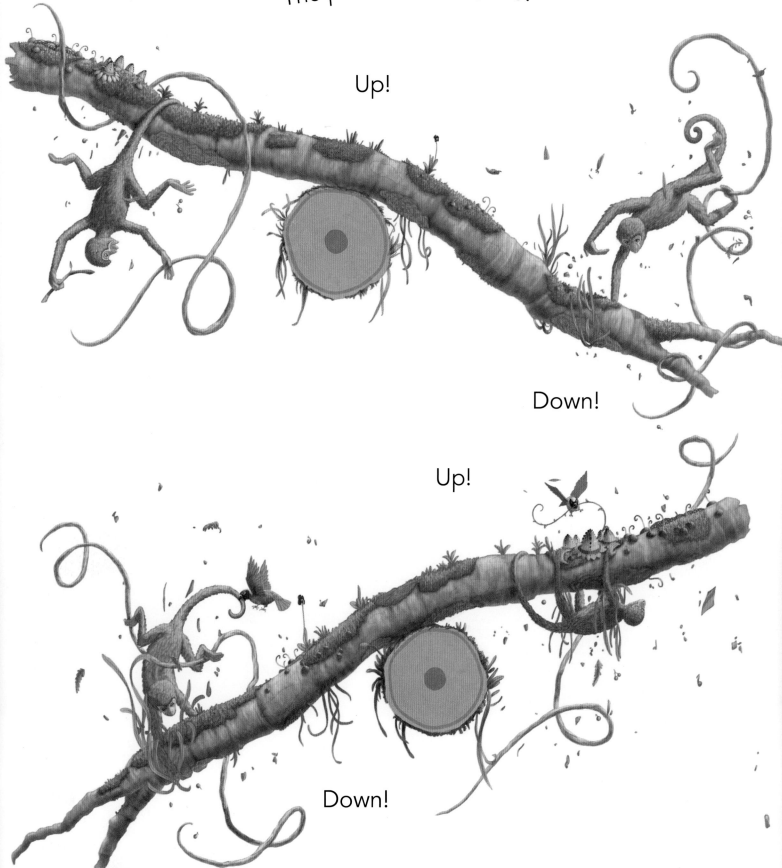

Down!

Up!

Down!

But the lizards were happy just to watch.

"I declare," said Josephine.
"Are you blending with me?"

"Can't help it," said Napoleon. "Chameleon."